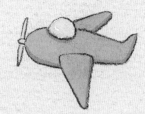

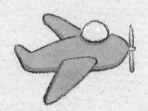

Sister and Me

Story and pictures by

Maple Lam

SCHOOL BUS

HARPER
An Imprint of HarperCollinsPublishers

For the very first time, Mom asks me to take my little sister home from the bus stop — all by myself!

She bounces and hops and sings
a song she learned from school.

"Take me home...
Country roads..."

I don't even know the song.
Maybe she is singing it wrong.

She picks up all sorts of trash on our way.

"Ewwwww."

She misses her teddy bear.

"Did you bring Teddy with
you to school this morning?"

"No."

"Can you wait until we get home?"

She thinks about it.

"Okay."

She chases after a big dog
five times her size,

but hides behind me when
the baby squirrels squeal.

Then she has to use the potty.

"Do you absolutely
need to, right now?"

"Ummm..."

"Can you wait until we get home?"

She thinks about it.

"Okay."

We play medieval knights with
branches we found on the ground.

"What a rain cloud!
Let's get going."

"Come on . . ."

Sigh.

"No, no, no!"

"SLOW DOWN!"

"Wait up! Wait up!
It's just a thunderstorm!"

"Here. Give me
your hand."

"Be careful."

"Let's get out
of the rain."

I clean her hand.

"I did not cry.
I am really brave."

"Yes, you are."

She teaches me the song while we wait for the rain cloud to go away.

The sky clears, and we
head out once again.

When we get home,
Mom hugs and kisses us.

She is so proud.

We have a very relaxing afternoon.

After dinner, I receive a special present.

You are the best big brother, and you are very brave.

"Yes, I am."

The End

My Little Sister and Me

Copyright © 2016 by Maple Lam

All rights reserved. Manufactured in China.

No part of this book may be used or reproduced in any manner whatsoever without written permission except
in the case of brief quotations embodied in critical articles and reviews. For information address HarperCollins
Children's Books, a division of HarperCollins Publishers, 195 Broadway, New York, NY 10007.

www.harpercollinschildrens.com

ISBN 978-0-06-239697-6

The artist used colored pencils and watercolor to create the illustrations for this book.

Typography by Maple Lam and Dana Fritts

16 17 18 19 20 SCP 10 9 8 7 6 5 4 3 2 1

First Edition